On the Shoulder of A
GIANT

AN INUIT FOLKTALE

Published in Canada by Inhabit Media Inc. (www.inhabitmedia.com)

Inhabit Media Inc.
        (Iqaluit Office), P.O. Box 11125, Iqaluit, Nunavut, X0A 1H0
        (Toronto Office), 146A Orchard View Blvd., Toronto, Ontario, M4R 1C3

We acknowledge the support of the Canada Council for the Arts for our publishing program.

We acknowledge the support of the Government of Canada through the Department of Canadian Heritage Canada Book Fund program.

Printed and bound in Canada

Library and Archives Canada Cataloguing in Publication

Christopher, Neil, 1972-, author
        On the shoulder of a giant : an Inuit folktale / by Neil
Christopher ; illustrated by Jim Nelson.

ISBN 978-1-77227-002-0 (bound)

        1. Inuit--Folklore. I. Nelson, Jim, 1962-, illustrator
II. Title.

E99.E7C546475 2015   j398.209719'5   C2015-900418-7

ON THE SHOULDER OF A GIANT

AN INUIT FOLKTALE

RETOLD BY
NEIL CHRISTOPHER

ILLUSTRATED BY
JIM NELSON

INTRODUCTION

When I first arrived in the Arctic, everything was new to me—the land without trees, the frozen ocean, the winter storms, and the unique wildlife. But it was the stories that captured my attention so completely. I have always loved legends and myths. When I was a child, my parents would end the day with stories, and the stories with monsters and magic were my favourite. So, when northerners started sharing stories with me, I listened closely. And when I could not find anyone around to tell me more stories, I started spending time reading old books and archives. I wanted to learn more about the legends and myths from my Arctic home.

My favourite stories were the ones with giants in them. Over the years, as I encountered more and more stories, I began to notice how many stories involve giants. It seems that in ancient times the Arctic was home to many giants. But one giant in particular kept appearing in the stories of each Arctic region I explored. It was my research on this great giant that inspired this book. He is called by different names in each region, but he can be easily recognized, as he was the only giant who adopted an Inuit hunter as his son.

So, if there is only one Arctic giant story you take the time to learn about, this is the one to remember. And, if you are like me, this story will start your exploration into the world of Arctic giants. Have fun!

Neil Christopher
Iqaluit, Nunavut

From old stories passed forward from generation to generation, we know that long ago there lived a giant called Inukpak.🐦

Inukpak was huge, even for a giant. He was so tall that he could stride over the widest rivers and wade through the deepest lakes.

🐦 Pronounced "ee-newk-pak."

When Inukpak decided to travel, he could walk from one end of the Arctic to the other in just a few days.

When he arrived at a coast, he would wade far out into the sea to hunt for whales. Even if he walked out very far, the seawater would never come up past his knees.

One day, Inukpak met a hunter out on the tundra. Inukpak thought the little man looked friendly, and he did not want to frighten him. So, Inukpak crouched down very low and began to talk to the little person.

"Little child, why are you out here without your parents? Are you lost?" Inukpak said in his friendliest voice.

The hunter was terrified! He had never seen a giant before. And he did not understand why the giant had referred to him as a child, as he was an adult. But before the hunter could say anything or run away, Inukpak lifted the man up and put him on his shoulder.

"Don't worry, little son. I will look after you and bring you with me on my walk."

And, before the hunter could say a word, Inukpak started walking.

The hunter did not want to go on a walk, but what could he say to the giant?

Very soon, they were so far away from where they had started that the hunter did not know where they were or how to get home. The hunter looked around for anything he could recognize, but everything looked strange.

Eventually the hunter saw a lake so big that he could not see the other side. In fact, it was not a lake at all. It was the sea! The hunter lived inland, and he had never seen the sea before, so he did not recognize it for what it was.

Inukpak took the hunter off his shoulder and held him close to his face so they could talk.

"I am going to catch a sculpin for us to eat," the giant said. "But I don't think I should bring you into the water with me. You are too small, and if you fall into the water I might not be able to find you. I have never had a little son before, and I don't want to lose you."

The hunter wanted to explain to Inukpak that he was not a child, and that he did not need anyone to adopt him. But what could he say? He was so far away from where he lived, and he was not sure how to get home.

So, the hunter decided he should not upset Inukpak and he just said, "Okay."

Inukpak put the hunter on a pile of rocks and then waded far out into the sea.

The man watched the giant stand motionless in the water for some time. Suddenly, Inukpak plunged his hand into the sea and pulled out a huge whale.

"I got a sculpin! I got a sculpin!" Inukpak yelled.

Inukpak came running back to the beach, and his quick steps caused a huge wave to form. The little hunter tried to get out of the way, but the water was too fast and he was covered by the huge wave.

When Inukpak got to the beach, he looked around but did not see his little son.

"Little son, little son, where are you hiding?" Inukpak called.

Eventually, Inukpak noticed the little hunter lying in a big puddle of saltwater. Inukpak laughed and said, "There you are! You should not have played in the water. Now your caribou clothing is soaked! But don't worry, I have caught us a sculpin, so we will sleep with full bellies tonight!"

The hunter wanted to tell the giant that he had not been playing in the water. He also wanted to explain to Inukpak that he had caught a bowhead whale, not a sculpin. But, once again, the little hunter did not want to argue with a giant, so he just said, "Okay."

Inukpak began cutting up the whale, and the hunter looked for a sunny place to spread out his clothing to dry.

Suddenly, the hunter saw a huge polar bear coming toward him.

"Inukpak! INUKPAK!" the hunter yelled. "There is a polar bear! A polar bear!"

Inukpak jumped to his feet and looked in the direction of where his little son was pointing. Inukpak loved hunting bears, and he had not seen one in many years. But he could not see any polar bears in the area.

"Where is the polar bear, little son?" Inukpak asked. "Polar bears are very large, and I do not see any around."

The polar bear was coming closer to the hunter, and he was getting nervous. The hunter pointed at the bear and yelled to the giant, "The polar bear is right there!"

When Inukpak saw what the hunter was pointing at, the giant laughed and picked up the bear with two fingers. The polar bear growled and scratched the giant's hand, but this just made the giant laugh louder.

When Inukpak finally stopped laughing, he said to his son,
"This is not a polar bear. This is a baby fox or lemming. It
is much too small to be a polar bear!"

The hunter once again did not know what to say.
How could he argue with a giant?

Inukpak tossed the polar bear far into the sea and sat down to
eat his scuplin, which was really a bowhead whale.

After eating all he could, Inukpak lay down on the tundra and stared up at the sky. He took off his sealskin boots and placed them on the ground beside him.

"Goodnight, little son. You can sleep in my boot. It will keep you dry if it rains."

Then Inukpak yawned and fell asleep.

The hunter sat inside the boot and thought about his day. He had started out looking for caribou on the tundra, and now he was the son of a giant by the seacoast. The hunter thought about running away, but he didn't know where he was or how to get home. The giant seemed kind, so the hunter decided to stay with Inukpak and travel with him.

In time, the giant and the hunter became good friends. And the two of them travelled all across the North and had many adventures together.

And that is why, in every region of the Arctic, you can find stories about a huge giant who adopted a human!

MORE ABOUT
ARCTIC GIANTS

When you study giants, it is important to identify what kind of giants you are talking about. You might choose to categorize the various giants by their behaviour, such as friendly giants, cruel giants, etc., or by some other characteristic. However, I usually start by identifying a giant's size. In traditional Inuit stories there are two terms that you can use to categorize giants in this way.

The largest giants are called inukpasugjuit (pronounced "ee-newk-pa-sug-you-eet"), or the great giants. The story you just read is about a great giant. These giants are the size of mountains, and they are incredibly powerful. They are so large that they do not see the world as we do. A huge animal, like a bowhead whale, might seem like a little fish to these great giants. They do not usually bother with humans much, as we are so small and insignificant to the great giants.

HUMAN

INUKPASUGJUK
(GREAT GIANT)

INUGARULIGASUGJUK
(LESSER GIANT)

There is a category of smaller giants called
inugaruligasugjuit (pronounced "ee-new-ga-rul-lee-ga-sug-
you-eet"), or the lesser giants. These giants are about
two to three times the size of an adult human. Some
lesser giants look like very large humans, and others
have a strange appearance, like an ogre or a
troll. Inugaruligasugjuit are very strong. Some
of these lesser giants are kind and helpful,
but most are dangerous and cruel.

There are very few great giants left in the
world. And that is probably a good thing, as
they can knock down mountains or cause
tidal waves by accident.
These great giants
usually live alone,
as they often do
not get along with
each other. So, in
the rare instances
when they do
encounter one
another, it
usually ends in
a terrible fight.

It is said that in the remote regions of the High Arctic there live great wind giants. The male wind giants are huge, powerful, and cruel. It is said that the cold Arctic winds and storms originate in the land of the northern wind giants.

If a traveller mistakenly arrives in the land of the wind giants, these huge beings will hurl boulders at the visitor, as they do not like to be disturbed.

All giants love to hunt and fish. And for the great giants, their favourite animals to hunt are the giant polar bears, called nanurluit (plural form, pronounced "nan-oor-loo-eet"). For the great giants, there is no other prey that can match their size and strength like a nanurluk (singular form, pronounced "nan-oor-look").

It has been suggested that the great giants have almost hunted all of these giant polar bears into extinction and that there are very few left in the world. This is why we rarely hear about the nanurluit. But, occasionally, a hunter who ventures far from his community will come back with a story about seeing an enormous polar bear.

According to legends, a nanurluk spends most of its time in the sea. Occasionally nanurluit might be seen on land, but they usually stay close to the shore.

One of the reasons that we no longer see giants could be that they are sleeping. Sometimes, when the great giants get tired, they fall into a very deep sleep. And, when great giants sleep deeply, it can take centuries before they wake up.

Elders have said that while great giants are sleeping, dirt and gravel can settle on them, and plants and lichens can start growing all over them.

Some people believe that many of the mountains in the Arctic are actually sleeping giants that could one day wake up!

ABOUT THE AUTHOR AND ILLUSTRATOR

NEIL CHRISTOPHER is an educator, author, and filmmaker. He first moved to the North many years ago to help start a high school program in Resolute Bay, Nunavut. It was those students who first introduced Neil to the mythical inhabitants from Inuit traditional stories. The time spent in Resolute Bay changed the course of Neil's life. Since that first experience in the Arctic, Nunavut has been the only place he has been able to call home. For the last sixteen years, Neil has worked with many community members to record and preserve traditional Inuit stories. Together with his colleague, Louise Flaherty, and his brother, Danny Christopher, Neil started a small publishing company in Nunavut called Inhabit Media Inc. and has since been working to promote northern stories and authors.

JIM NELSON is a freelance artist based in Chicago, Illinois. He has a lifelong interest in myths, legends, and the fantastic.

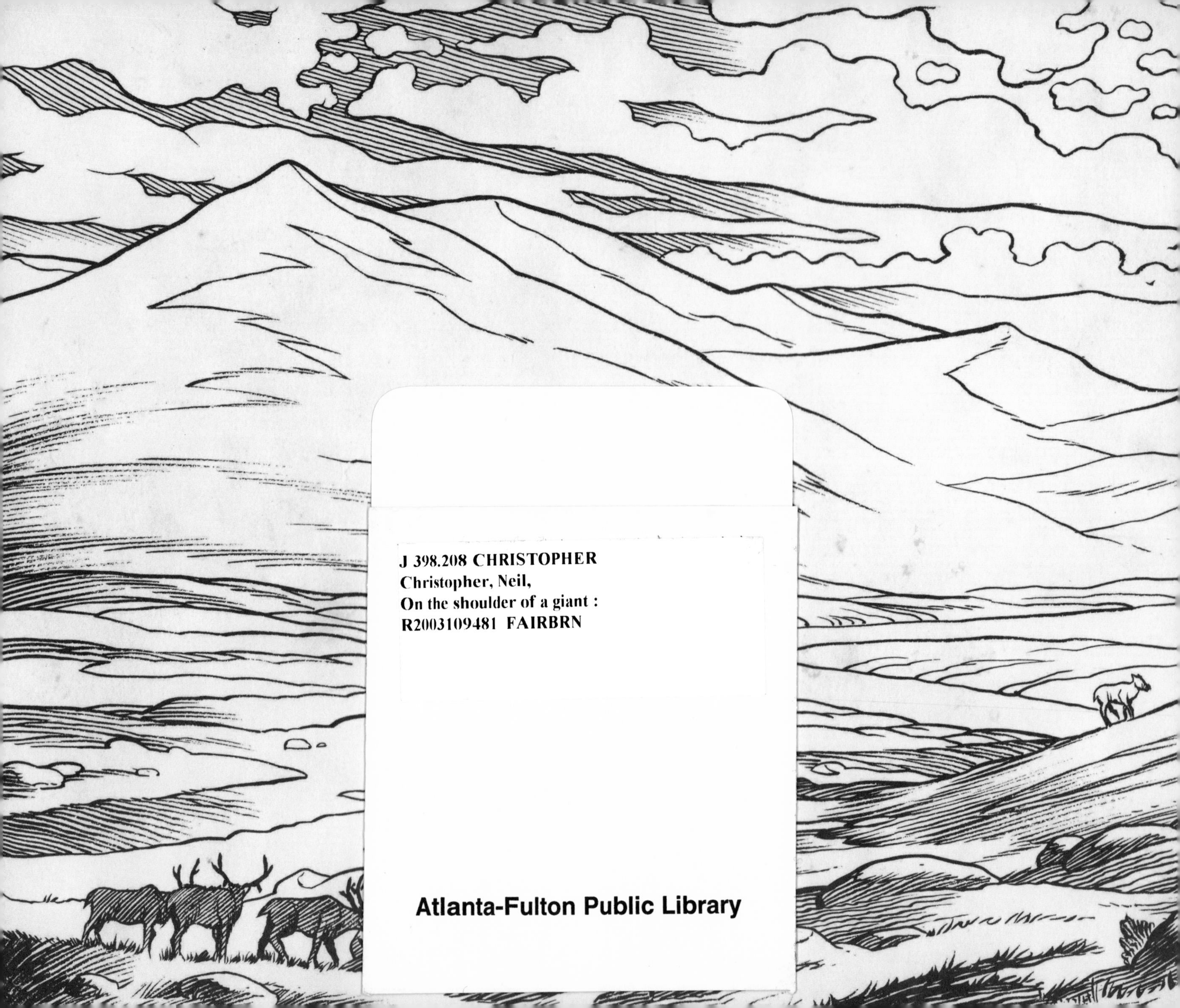